BL 2.4   AR 0.5= ½^{pt}

11/06

DEMCO

MRS. WATSON
WANTS YOUR TEETH

STORY BY

Alison McGhee

PICTURES BY

Harry Bliss

Harcourt, Inc.

Orlando Austin New York San Diego Toronto London

www.HarcourtBooks.com

Library of Congress Cataloging-in-Publication Data
McGhee, Alison, 1960–
Mrs. Watson wants your teeth/by Alison McGhee; pictures by Harry Bliss.
p. cm.
Summary: A first grader is frightened on her first day of school
after hearing a rumor that her teacher is a 300-year-old
alien with a purple tongue who steals baby teeth from her students.
[1. Schools—Fiction. 2. First day of school—Fiction.
3. Teachers—Fiction. 4. Teeth—Fiction.]
I. Bliss, Harry, 1964– ill. II. Title.
PZ7.M4784675Mr 2004
[E]—dc22 2003021267
ISBN 0-15-204931-2

C E G H F D B

Printed in Singapore

The pictures in this book were done in black ink
and watercolor on Arches 90 lb. watercolor paper.
The display lettering was created by Jane Dill.
The text type was hand-lettered by Paul Colin.
Color separations by Bright Arts Ltd., Hong Kong
Printed and bound by Tien Wah Press, Singapore
This book was printed on totally chlorine-free Stora Enso Matte paper.
Production supervision by Sandra Grebenar and Ginger Boyer
Designed by Suzanne Fridley and Scott Piehl

For Min O'Brien
—A. M.

For my hilarious, toothless,
hockey-playing son, Alex
—H. B.

I have a secret....

First grade begins today, and I'm in BIG trouble.

It's a known fact that Mrs. Watson, the first-grade teacher, is a three-hundred-year-old alien who steals baby teeth from her students.

How do I know? A second grader told me.

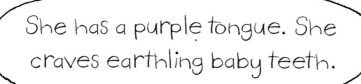

My secret? I have a loose tooth! It's my first one.

It's so loose that every time I take a bite, I expect it to fall right out.

I miss my kindergarten teacher. She was the one who taught me how to tie my shoes.

I did it!

She let me bring stuffed animals to class.

And she did *not* have a "treat box" or a purple tongue.

PINK

MRS. WATSON'S LOST TOOTH GALLERY 1990 —
WHO WILL IT BE THIS YEAR ?!
MRS. WATSON
L.A.
NEW YORK
TEXAS

LATER...

I want to get a good look at Mrs. Watson's purple tongue . . .

and those earrings . . .

and her "pearl" necklace. . . .

At snack time, I look up. Guess who is right there?

It's going to be a long year—a long, silent, snackless, tooth-protecting year.

At recess, I look up. Guess who's right there?

BACK IN CLASS...

Does that boy know that Mrs. Watson is really a three-hundred-year-old alien with a purple tongue who needs earthling baby teeth in order to survive? I have to warn him!

Mrs. Watson comes toward *me* with the treat box!

And that's when it happens. . . .

I get a good look at Mrs. Watson's pearl necklace...

and her earrings...

and I get an extra good look at the treat box!